SECRETS AND STRAYS

SECRETS
AND
STRAYS

By Gwendolyn Lavert

Illustrated by April M. Ward

 **Wright Group**
McGraw-Hill

Secrets and Strays
D-MAN AND BEANS SERIES

Text copyright ©2002 by Gwendolyn B. Lavert
Illustrations copyright ©2002 by April M. Ward

Published by Wright Group/McGraw-Hill,
a division of the McGraw-Hill Companies, Inc.

Wright Group/McGraw-Hill
19201 120th Avenue NE, Suite 100
Bothell, WA 98011
www.WrightGroup.com

Printed in China through Colorcraft Ltd., Hong Kong

10 9 8 7 6 5 4 3 2 1

ISBN: 0-322-06248-9
ISBN: 0-322-06258-6 (6-pack)

SECRETS AND STRAYS

CHAPTER ONE

"Benita! Benita! Benita Kelly!"

Beans heard Mrs. King, her English teacher. But she didn't answer. She wasn't used to being called Benita. Everyone but Mrs. King used her nickname. Mrs. King was the only one who refused to call her Beans.

"Earth to Benita Kelly!"

"Oh! Yes, Mrs. King," said Beans, "were you talking to me?"

"I was, young lady." Mrs. King tapped on her

book and gave Beans a stern look. "I'd like you to read the last paragraph," she said.

"What page was that?" asked Beans, flipping through her book.

"Page eighty-nine," said Mrs. King.

Beans was nervous. She just sat there. Her pencil shook. She twisted in her seat. The book fell to the floor with a thump. Then she stammered, "I can't find my-my gl-glasses."

Some of the kids snickered.

Dooley Delray, called D-man by his basketball team friends, sat next to Beans. He started tapping on the edge of his desk. "Who are you trying to fool?" he asked in a loud whisper. "Everyone knows you can't read. That's the real deal."

"D-man, you are such a nerd! You don't know what you're talking about," Beans whispered back.

The class started buzzing.

"That's enough," said Mrs. King. "I will not have this disruption. Beans, you need to bring your glasses to school every day. Class participation is very important."

Beans scowled at the smirk on Dooley's face. Then she looked out the window. Beyond the playground fence she saw boarded-up houses. Between the houses she saw leaves dancing in the autumn wind. Dancing—that's what she wanted to be doing. Tap dancing her way to Broadway. Not sitting in this boring class.

The bell rang.

Mrs. King said, "Class is dismissed. Dooley, I need to see you about your report!"

"Uh, Mrs. King," said Dooley, moving toward her desk, "I'm gonna be late for class."

Everybody rushed busily out the door. Beans eyed the sketchpad on Dooley's desk. Then she walked by. Beans quickly picked up the sketch-pad. She stuck it between her books. Her heart was racing. She headed out the door.

What should I do? What should I do?

Before she knew it, she was in front of the girls' bathroom. She went in and ducked into a stall. Nervously, she opened the sketchpad. She flipped through pages of cartoon characters. Dooley was always bragging about his cartoons. Then came drawings of cats. There were sleek cats, fat cats, scrawny cats.

Not bad for a nerd, she thought.

Three thick rubber bands hugged the rest of the

pages closed. Carefully, Beans removed the rubber bands. This was definitely not stuff Dooley had ever bragged about. Beans saw pictures of a kid with wings sitting on a big, fluffy cloud. He was looking down toward earth. It was a picture of Dooley, she

guessed. But he looked sad and small.

Next came a drawing of a funeral procession.

Beans remembered the days Dooley had been absent for his grandmother's funeral. When he came back to school he was so quiet. She'd caught him several times looking out the window.

Beans looked at the angel picture again. Dooley made a funny angel. She could see why he wanted to hide it. He couldn't brag about it. Everybody would tease him. Maybe feel sorry for him. Whatever! The worse the better. Nothing could be worse than what he did to her. She just wanted to pay him back.

She pushed the sketchpad down into her backpack and left the bathroom. In the hallway, she saw Dooley. He came right up to her.

"I know you took my sketchpad," he said.

"That's your opinion," Beans said.

"If I find out you did," said Dooley, "I'll make you sorry!"

"I double dare you!" said Beans.

"Yeah, like I'm scared or something!" Dooley smirked.

Mrs. King walked up to them.

"Benita, Dooley, what is going on here? Never mind. Just get to class."

CHAPTER TWO

For the rest of the day, Beans watched the clock.

When the final bell rang, she raced from her seat.

"Wait up!" called her good friend Mandy. "I'll walk home with you."

"No!" said Beans, "I've got something to do today."

"What?" asked Mandy.

"Things!" said Beans.

"You've found another best friend?" asked Mandy.

"Mandy!" said Beans. "Please! I'll see you tomorrow." Mandy would ask too many questions.

She didn't want to have to answer any questions right now.

Beans ran quickly out of the school. She walked home in a daze. She didn't notice the weed-infested yards. She passed boarded-up store fronts without seeing them. She barely even noticed the earthshaking dance music blasting from the second-floor windows on South Rampart Street. She ignored the steady flow of people as she passed the stores and restaurants on Main Street: Glover's Barber Shop, Cute & Sassy Beauty Salon, Amy and Lou's

Fine Restaurant, and Smitty's Dry Cleaning.

"Benita! Benita! Como estás?" Mrs. Sanchez stood in a yard filled with many pots, pans, and vases. She was known as the junk lady. Her business was called "The Bazaar."

"Look what I found today. It is a treasure." Mrs. Sanchez held up a handbag made of deep blue satin. It was covered with dyed-to-match pearls.

"It's beautiful!" said Beans. She looked past the handbag.

"Are you okay?" asked Mrs. Sanchez. "Where's that smile?" She took off one of her bright bead necklaces. She put it around Beans's neck. "You need one of these!" she said. "It will cheer you up."

"Nothing will!" said Beans, "except Dooley Delray disappearing."

"Disappearing!" said Mrs. Sanchez. "I'm surprised at you."

"He makes me mad!" said Beans.

Mrs. Sanchez pulled Beans to her. "Now, tell me," said Mrs. Sanchez, hugging her tightly, "It will make you feel better."

Tears welled up in Beans's eyes. "D-man started a rumor," said Beans. "He lied about me."

"Are you sure about that?" asked Mrs. Sanchez.

"He said I couldn't read!" said Beans. "But I'm going to fix him."

"Now Beans," said Mrs. Sanchez, "remember the Golden Rule. Do unto others. . . ."

". . . as you want them to do unto you. I know that!" said Beans. "But he hurt me today."

"Two wrongs don't make a right," said Mrs. Sanchez.

"I'm tired of him bragging about his cartoons. He's not the best artist. I've seen better. After what I saw today, I can make it bad for him. He'll never show his sketchpad again. I'll tell his little secret."

"Benita Kelly!" said Mrs. Sanchez sternly. "Secrets can be good or bad. If you tell Dooley's secret and it hurts him, that's a bad kind of secret."

"I don't care!" said Beans. She looked into Mrs. Sanchez's picture window and saw Mrs. Sanchez's cat. She yelled, "Mrs. Sanchez! Look, it's Sasha! She's jumped from the piano and now she's pawing at the curtains."

"Sasha!" called Mrs. Sanchez.

"What's that terrible smell coming from your

house?" asked Beans.

"Oh, my goodness! My supper! It's burning!" exclaimed Mrs. Sanchez.

"I'll help!" shouted Beans.

Beans ran around to the back of the house and into the kitchen. Her eyes watered from the smoke. She quickly turned off the burner. With a potholder, she pulled the pot off the stove. The bad smell of the burning pot made her nose itch. She carried the smoking pot outside to the patio table.

"Chiquita, thank you! Are you all right?"

"I'm fine," said Beans, "but your dinner isn't."

"You saved my kitchen and Sasha. That's more important." Mrs. Sanchez and Beans looked down at Sasha. The cat rubbed up against Mrs. Sanchez's leg. Mrs. Sanchez reached down and picked her up. She stroked her thick fur.

"Poor Sasha. I've been afraid to let her out for fresh air. Those wild cats keep coming around. I don't want them running after her."

Beans looked at Mrs. Sanchez. She was usually so lively. Now her face seemed gray. She looked every bit of her seventy years.

"Don't worry about your supper, Mrs. Sanchez," Beans said. "Mama always cooks too much. I'll bring you dinner."

"Muchas gracias. That's very kind of you," said

Mrs. Sanchez. "I'm going in to air out the house."

Beans crossed the street to her house. Walking up the steps, she stopped in her tracks. There sat a cat on her doorstep. It seemed to be waiting for her.

"Hello!" said Beans. "Where did you come from?"

Beans moved toward the cat. He stood there. She reached down and softly smoothed back his fur. She stroked his ears.

"You are a friendly little thing," said Beans, "Do you have a home?"

Meow! Meow! Meow!

"You're hungry," said Beans, picking him up.

She'd never been allowed to have a cat. Mama thought they cost too much and clawed the furniture. So Beans had to be content with stuffed cats and books about cats and playing with Sasha.

She remembered Mrs. Sanchez's words about the wild cats. She pulled the cat closer.

"Wild cats! You're not wild," she whispered. "It's all right, little one. I'll figure out a way to get Mama

to let me keep you. Even if I don't tell her about you just yet. You'll be my little secret for awhile."

Suddenly, Mrs. Sanchez's words buzzed in her mind like bumblebees in a jar. "Secrets can be good or bad."

This time, Beans had a good secret. She slipped the cat into her backpack next to the sketchpad.

CHAPTER THREE

The aroma from the kitchen met her at the door.

"Mama!" she called. "I'm home."

"Hey! Beans, I'm in the kitchen," she said.

"I'm going to take my backpack to my room. I'll be right back."

"Are you hungry?" asked Mama.

"Starved!" said Beans.

"Good!" said Mama. "I've made a ton of spaghetti and meat sauce."

Beans went into the small bedroom she shared

with her mother and closed the door. She eased the sleeping cat out of her backpack. She put him on her favorite pillow. Next came the sketchpad. She pulled off her sweater and put it on top of the sketchpad. Then Beans left the room, closing the door behind her.

Walking into the kitchen, she hugged her mama. "Thanks for cooking my favorite tonight," she said.

"I'm glad that you made noodles. May I take some over to Mrs. Sanchez?"

"Sure," said Mama, "but why?"

"Mrs. Sanchez had a fire in her kitchen just now."

"A fire!" said Mama.

"Yes. I was talking to her and then I smelled something burning. So I ran around to the back. I went inside and took the pot off the burner," said Beans.

"Benita!" said Mama, "I'm so proud of you. Was Mrs. Sanchez hurt?"

"No, but I don't think she should be cooking. She looked pretty upset."

"Mrs. Sanchez has done a lot for this community. We will do anything to help her."

"Well, I'm going to start my homework," said Beans.

Beans went back to her room. She closed the door and turned on the music. It vibrated around the

room. She clapped her hands and moved her feet.
Beans loved to perform. Dooley didn't have to tell
her or the whole class that she was bad at reading.
She already knew that. But nobody could ever tell
her that she couldn't dance.

Then Beans picked up the cat and began to
dance. Now, she had a partner. Her shoulders
shook. Her hips wiggled.

"I need a name for you," said Beans. "You are
strong. You are a traveler."

Her braids swung back and forth. Beans swirled

around and around.

"You will protect me," said Beans. "I'll call you Nelson."

Knock! Knock! Knock!

"Beans! Beans!" called Mama. "Dinner is ready."

Beans couldn't hear. She moved to the rhythm of the music. Suddenly, she stood face to face with her mama.

"Benita!" said Mama. "What are you doing with a cat in this house?"

Beans lost her balance. She fell on the bed. Well, one secret was out! thought Beans.

"Mama!" said Beans. "Before you get mad, let me explain."

"It better be good, young lady," said Mama.

"Well, see . . . " said Beans, ". . . after I saved Mrs. Sanchez's house, I came home. I found Nelson on our porch."

"So, you've given him a name," said Mama.

"No!" said Beans. "Well, yes! I guess. It just came to me. I like the name Nelson."

"All right, young lady," said Mama.

"Does that mean I can keep him?" asked Beans.

"Stray cats are roamers. They never stay in one place very long. They don't like to be caged in."

"This one is different. Look how cute he is," said Beans. "He knows that I love him. He'll never leave."

Beans picked him up and followed her mama to the kitchen. Mama looked from Nelson to Beans.

"Okay," said Mama, "for tonight only! Now, take Mrs. Sanchez her dinner. It'll get cold."

"Thank you!" Beans gave her mama a big hug.

"Stay," Beans whispered to Nelson as she opened the door. She looked back as she walked down the steps. She saw Nelson through the screen door. "No slipping off! You're all mine."

As Beans crossed the street, she saw Dooley. "Dooley! Dooley!" she called. "Wait! I want to talk to you."

He turned around. "Leave me alone, I've got to get home," he said. "I've looked everywhere. I can't find my sketchpad. I've got one more place to look."

Then he started running.

"D-man, wait! Come back!"

"No!" he shouted.

Beans stood watching him run faster and faster. If he'd only waited. She was going to get the sketchpad.

She rang Mrs. Sanchez's doorbell.

"Oh, Chiquita! You are so special." Mrs. Sanchez smiled as she took the plate. "Why such a long face?"

"I just saw Dooley, but he wouldn't talk to me," said Beans.

"You will see him tomorrow," said Mrs. Sanchez. "You will make it right. You will be friends. Trust me."

Mrs. Sanchez gave her a hug. Little drops of rain began to fall. Beans ran across the street, up the steps, and into the house for her dinner. She found Nelson, curled up near the door. Nelson was home.

CHAPTER FOUR

Beans walked into the classroom. She heard Dooley bragging. This time it was about some cat. She quickly took her seat.

"Girl!" said Mandy, "where have you been? I waited for you."

"I've got a cat," whispered Beans.

"D-man got one, too!" said Mandy.

"I heard," said Beans. "Who cares?"

"Well, you're in a super mood today," said Mandy.

"I've got a cat who loves me," said Beans.

Dooley was looking in her direction.

"Everybody's been talking about a big fight!" said Mandy. "Tell me it's not true."

Beans leaned back and said, "Rumors! Rumors! Rumors!"

The tardy bell sounded. Dooley slid into his seat. Beans sat like a statue. She didn't breathe. She kept her eyes down. She wasn't called on. At last, the class ended.

Dooley gave her a nasty look. "I'll see you at

lunch," he said. He disappeared into the crowd. She went to her locker, shaking. This whole thing with Dooley was out of control.

She opened her backpack. She pulled out a taped-up packet. She put it in the back of the locker. She locked the door. The bell rang.

Beans went to Language Arts. Now she had to write a report on pioneer life. The words weren't coming. Why couldn't she write about dance? She

knew everything about dance. She especially loved tap dancing. She knew all about the great tappers. She could fill several pages.

"Beans," said Mrs. Francis, "I want you to take your paper home and finish it. You can bring it back tomorrow."

"Thanks, Mrs. Francis."

Beans put her books in her backpack and slowly left the room. Now it was lunchtime. She knew he'd be in the cafeteria. If she fought, she'd be suspended. She'd never been in a fight. Fighting wasn't her style. She turned the corner. There stood Dooley.

"Give it to me now!" said Dooley. "I know you have it."

Beans just stood there. Frozen. Dooley moved closer to her. This wasn't the time to confess. This wasn't the place. Everybody would think she was a thief.

"Get away from her!" shouted Mandy. "Leave

her alone. Get out of her face. You've done enough already."

"Me!" said Dooley. "So, you're going to take up for your little friend?"

Mandy took Beans by the arm. They pushed past Dooley. Beans felt numb.

"You haven't heard the last of this," said Dooley.

Mandy led Beans to a back table in the cafeteria. That's just like Mandy, thought Beans. She was looking after Beans. But only Beans could rescue herself.

Away from listening ears, Mandy asked, "Do you have Dooley's sketchpad?"

"I don't want to talk about it," said Beans. "Even though you're my best friend."

Beans knew that Mandy was hurt, but she couldn't get her involved. Beans didn't know what to do. Nothing was working out.

I've got to give the sketchpad back! I'm sick of

this mess! thought Beans. I didn't mean for it to go this far.

The last period of the day was homeroom. Mrs. King went over the announcements. Beans heard her name.

"We are looking for help with a class project. Benita's mother called. She told me about Mrs. Sanchez's kitchen fire. I want the class to know that Benita put out that fire."

The class cheered and clapped. Beans sat very still.

"I think that she can get the services of City Meals-on-Wheels."

"My neighbor gets those meals," said Dooley. "They deliver meals right to your home."

"That's right," said Mrs. King.

"What's our part?" asked Mandy.

"That's a good question," said Mrs. King. "Our class will volunteer to help Mrs. Sanchez in The Bazaar."

"There's a problem," said Beans. "Mrs. Sanchez will think this is a handout."

"Benita," asked Mrs. King, "do you think you can convince her to let us help?"

"I'll do my best," said Beans.

CHAPTER FIVE

Beans walked home, glad that the day was over. Mrs. Sanchez was helping a customer, but she waved at Beans.

"How's the secret?" she called.

"Awful!" said Beans.

Beans stayed until all the customers were gone. She dusted the glassware. She rearranged the handbags.

"You do such a great job, Beans," said Mrs. Sanchez. "I could use someone every day."

"That's a great idea!" said Beans. "Mrs.

Sanchez, our class is looking for a school project. We can help you. Every day."

"Just today, I talked with the Meals-on-Wheels people about bringing my dinner. While I'm eating, you kids can look after my customers. When can you start?"

"Today," said Beans. "Mama's going to send your supper over tonight."

"You are too kind, my dear friend." Mrs. Sanchez wiped her eyes.

Beans went home. She found Nelson waiting for her. He was curled up on her favorite pillow. He followed Beans into the kitchen.

"Thanks, Mama, for letting Nelson stay," said Beans, as she opened a can of tuna.

"Only until we can find him a good home," said Mama. "Until then, he must stay off the furniture."

"I promise, promise, promise!" said Beans. She gave her mama a long hug.

"Enough, enough!" said Mama. She hugged Beans tightly.

"Mrs. Sanchez's dinner is ready," said Mama. "You can take it over."

"Okay!" said Beans. "Nelson, you stay here and finish your dinner."

With the covered dish in her hands, Beans crossed the street. She rang the doorbell.

Mrs. Sanchez came to the door just as a car

pulled up in her driveway. D-man got out with a huge package.

"What are you doing here?" asked Beans. "Today isn't your day."

"My mom said it was," said Dooley.

"Come in. Come in. Both of you," said Mrs. Sanchez. "Nothing will go to waste."

Mrs. Sanchez opened the door wide. Beans walked in. Something brushed against her leg. It was a cat. Mrs. Sanchez swirled around. Dooley lunged for it, but the cat leapt onto Mrs. Sanchez's antique piano from Mexico. Sasha was resting on top. Then Beans recognized the new cat.

"Nelson!" she said. "How did you get out?"

Then Dooley recognized the cat. "Peppers!" he said. "Where have you been? You didn't come home last night. I've looked everywhere for you."

"No, that's my Nelson!" said Beans.

"Well, Nelson. Or is it Peppers?" asked Mrs. Sanchez, laughing. "Looks like you've been playing

a game." The cat just purred happily.

"He's mine!" said Beans.

"He's mine, too," said Dooley.

"Let's stop the arguing," said Mrs. Sanchez. "Let's talk."

"I don't want to talk to her," said Dooley. "I want my sketchpad back. I know Beans took it."

"Why would she do that?" asked Mrs. Sanchez.

"Anybody could have taken it," said Beans. "You're always bragging about it, I know a lot of people who can draw better than you."

"You were the last to leave the class. When I went back to my desk, my pad was gone."

"And," said Beans, "that's not reason enough for me to take the sketchpad."

"Well," said Dooley, hanging his head, "I know that I embarrassed you. Talking about your reading and all."

Beans stood there for a moment looking first at Mrs. Sanchez, then at Dooley.

"Maybe you didn't take it," said Dooley. "I was mean to you. I thought you wanted to get back at me. I just want my pictures back. They mean a lot to me."

"I'll be right back," said Beans.

"Where are you going?" asked Dooley. "You do a great job of walking away."

"You'll see!" said Beans. "Please! Just don't leave

until I get back."

Beans left Dooley holding Nelson/Peppers. She ran across the street to her house.

When she returned, she was carrying the taped-up package.

"Here," she said.

Dooley knew what it was. He tore the brown paper off. There was his sketchpad.

"I was wrong to have taken it," said Beans. "I tried to return it. Things just kept getting worse."

"I know," said Dooley. He looked down at Peppers. "I'm sorry."

Dooley stuck out his hand. Beans shook it.

"You got what you wanted," said Beans. "You're happy. Now, let me have Nelson."

"He's been with me longer!" said Dooley. "You've only had him for a night."

Nelson leapt off the piano. He settled at Mrs. Sanchez's feet.

"He seems quite happy here," said Mrs. Sanchez.

Beans and Dooley looked at each other.

"I've got it!" said Beans. "He can stay with Mrs. Sanchez and Sasha. We can visit him every day."

"We can feed him and play with him,"

"Can he stay?" asked Beans and Dooley, looking at Mrs. Sanchez. "That way, we can both have him."

"Okay!" said Mrs. Sanchez. "I can't promise he'll stay forever. He's a roamer. He has seen more of this city than the three of us."

"See!" said Beans.

"More!" said Dooley.

"Are you thinking what I'm thinking?" asked Beans.

"Yeah!" said Dooley. "A new name."

"Seymour!" they both chimed in.

"That's a wonderful name," said Mrs. Sanchez.

Seymour twitched his long tail. He knew he had two owners.

"He'll never be lonely with you two," said